For Anais, who has always known the truth. MM

For Jan Potter – for everything we shared. MJ & HP

First published in 2010
by Walker Books Australia Pty Ltd
Locked Bag 22, Newtown
NSW 2042 Australia
www.walkerbooks.com.au

National Library of Australia
Cataloguing-in-Publication entry:

McKinlay, Meg.

The truth about penguins / Meg McKinlay; illustrator, Mark Jackson.

ISBN: 978 1 921150 48 7 (hbk.)

For children.

Subjects: Penguins—Juvenile fiction
Other Authors/Contributors: Jackson, Mark.
A823.4

Typeset in Aunt Mildred
Printed and bound in China

2 4 6 8 10 9 7 5 3 1

P1-3

THE TRUE
PENG

Falkirk Council

MEG McKINLAY & MARK JACKSON

WALKER BOOKS
AND SUBSIDIARIES

LONDON • BOSTON • SYDNEY • AUCKLAND

Down at the zoo,
there was excitement in the air.
The animals were all a-buzz,
and a-roar and a-twitter.
Because the penguins were coming ...
the penguins were coming!

Umm ... what's a penguin?

Penguins?
Everybody knows penguins!
They're ... small and round and sort of ... penguin-y.

Penguins, eh? They're birds, you know.
Wings, feathers, beaks, all that bird stuff.
And flying!
Oh, yes, you should see them soar!

I heard penguins fly south for the winter, to get
away from the cold. Thousands of lonely miles,
they travel – oh, the cruel, cruel distance! –
over oceans and forests, mountains and lakes,
never stopping, not once, except maybe ... well ...

Pizza! They stop for pizza!

Olives, pepperoni, double cheese.

I read it in a book.

They're all about the cheese, penguins.

And beaches.

Ah, the sun! The sand!

They can't get enough of it, those penguins.

All winter, they lie around on tropical beaches.

Lazy little critters, they are. I tried teaching
some to swim once, you know. They were all –
It's too cold! It's too deep! It's too wet!
Wanted kickboards, floaties, the whole bit.
Hopeless, really.

They wear cool bathers, though.
Oh, they're fabulous, penguins, in their spots and
their stripes, and their funky little beach ponchos.
Finally, we'll have some colour in this place!

And their babies are so cute! Some of them wear booties,
you know. And little woolly hats. That's how they stay warm,
stuck at home with their nannies, while their parents are off
sunbathing on tropical beaches. Poor little things.

Yeah, tell me about it.

My mother was a penguin. They're terrible parents.

All they ever want to do is eat pizza and hang out at the beach looking funky.

And throw parties! Penguins are total party animals ...
I mean, birds. Party birds! They'll be keeping us up
all night with their loud music and their crazy dancing.
It's going to be **wild** around here.

STOP!

You are crazy, all of you!

None of you knows anything about penguins.

I am a zookeeper. I am an expert on penguins.

So I will tell you the truth ...

The truth about penguins is that they are black and white. All of them. There are no spots or stripes or funky beach ponchos. Penguins cannot fly, and even if they could, they would not fly anywhere for the winter. Penguins love winter. They love the cold.

A penguin would never sunbathe on a tropical beach. He would dive in and swim quickly back to his icy home, without kickboards or floaties or lessons from a demented pelican.

And please!

Penguins do not eat pizza.

They eat sensible, healthy food,
like fish and squid and little
sea creatures. They stay close by their
chicks, warming them with their bodies.
There are no hats or booties,
and definitely no nannies.

Penguins are wonderful parents

with cute chicks which look
nothing at all like elephants.
Not even really small ones.

The truth about peguins
is that they are perfectly
respectable ice-loving,
fish-eating,
black-and-white birds.
Penguins are not crazy,
or lazy or funky.
They are sensible birds,
in sensible colours,
with sensible,
peaceful ways.

And that is the
real, honest truth
about penguins.

Really.